WARNING

This book contains adult language and violence. It may be considered offensive to some readers. This book is for sale to adults ONLY.

* * * * * * * * * * * * * * * * *

Please store your files wisely where they cannot be accessed by underage readers.

ISBN-13: 978-1773500775
ISBN-10: 1773500775

Other Books by Freddie Kim:

The Time Guardian Thriller Series

When the Time Guardian goes missing, it is up to Sonia to travel back to the past the rectify the future of humanity. Follow this epic tale of good versus evil in the battle to control Earth's destiny.

Stinger Jacked

The Free Humanity Movement (FHM) resistance hatches a plan to steal a Stinger Class assault ship from OmniClon Universal (OCU) and its alliance partner, the ka'Thar. With morale at an all-time low, Rogal and his team of misfits are sent on what could potentially be a suicide mission.

Get the latest update on new releases from the author at:

https://www.freddiekim.com/newsletter/

This book is Part Three of the "The Cyber Heist Files"

Book 1 – Cyber Heist

The entire financial industry of the World Government is at risk when a weaponized virus is covertly uploaded into the computer system. Faced with an imminent crisis, the government releases the whistle blower, Tyler Wilkens, in exchange for eradicating the virus that has infected their computer systems. Something malevolent is afoot and Wilkens is the best chance the government has to combat it.

Book 2 – Kill Code

When Tyler Wilkens fails to completely eradicate the virus, he is put back in prison and his competitor, another tech company, is tasked with finishing the job. As circumstances turn dire, Wilkens is released once again to do the government's bidding. But what he finds within the computer system is something ominous and unexpected. Will Wilkens be able to save the World Government from complete financial collapse?

Book 3 – Coup D'état

With the World Government ousted in the coup d'état, OmniClon Universal (OCU) attempts to take control over the world. Tasked with finding evidence to save the former government, Wilkens falls deep down the rabbit hole. With the help of Monica Franchette, Wilkens uncovers a conspiracy that leads him to multiple assassinations and the highest levels of authority. The burden of truth does not come without its risks. Will Wilkens be a marked man with a target on his back for the rest of his life?

The Cyber Heist Files

Coup D'état

Book Three

By Freddie Kim

Copyright Revelry Publishing 2020

Table of Contents

Chapter One

THE COCKROACH scuttled silently along the baseboard and up to the sink. It cautiously explored the toothbrush with its undulating feelers. Satisfied with its destination, it lay a sticky, viscous transparent egg-like mass within the bristles.

After finishing its task, the critter crawled back down the sink and disappeared behind the baseboard. Within the walls, hidden away from prying eyes, the cockroach convulsed and rolled on its back, legs up. A tiny plume of smoke emerged from its thorax as an enzyme pouch erupted from within. In mere moments, the cockroach body disintegrated into a desiccated exoskeleton.

The alarm went off at the usual time of 4:30 AM. Before the second alarm cycle had a chance to sound off, a hand slapped down on the bedside clock, thus ending its morning rant.

The man made a slight groan before sitting up and rubbing his face to clear his eyes. Sliding into his slippers, he stood and shuffled into the bathroom. The face looking back from the mirror showed lines of weariness, cut deep from too many difficult decisions made over the years.

Turning on the faucet and applying some toothpaste, he brushed his teeth as he had done so many mornings before. Except that this time, something was different. A sharp pain emanated from the left side of his chest. The intense pain exploded unnaturally fast. He stumbled to the floor and was dead before his head hit the porcelain rim of the toilet.

Chapter Two

Tyler Wilkens had just settled into his window seat on a full flight. He was flying on the shuttle to make it home in time to attend his daughter's recital. Since being released from prison, he was determined to become more involved in her life. And that included participating in her extracurricular activities.

His daughter, Sterling, showed exceptional promise with the viola and she was so excited when Wilkens told her on the video call that he was attending her performance. But something nagged at Wilkens from within his core. His unhindered freedom seemed too good to be true, and he tried to force it from his mind before it became a self-fulfilling prophecy.

Although he had succeeded in eradicating the virus from the World Government's computer system, the win had come too late and at great cost. The World Government missed a crucial debt payment to OmniClon Universal (OCU) and now had to face substantial penalties. The specter of Clarence's death also weighed heavily on his shoulders. Clarence Rainer, the Systems Supervisor, was an administrator, not a fighter. The government bureaucrats had insisted that Clarence accompany Wilkens on his mission despite the risks.

None of those things was Wilkens' fault, but the ominous feeling he was experiencing came to a head. Three black sedans, with lights flashing and sirens blaring, rushed onto the tarmac and blocked the plane from approaching the runway.

After what seemed like hours, four agents, dressed in black suits and sunglasses, boarded the plane. The lead agent spoke to one of the flight attendants. She pointed down the aisle, and all eyes fell on Wilkens.

Here we go again. Wilkens slumped down in his seat, trying to look small. The disappointed look on his daughter's face flashed through his mind, and it broke his heart. He hoped she would forgive him. He knew what was coming next.

Felix Switzer, the Assistant Attorney General, sat across the table from Wilkens, who had remained chained to it for the past hour. They stared at each other for some time before Switzer spoke.

"You're in deep shit."

"Don't tell me. Let me guess. You're blaming me for the failings of the World Government's effort to make the last payment," said Wilkens with a sigh and a smirk.

"You think this is a joke? You'll get life for Clarence's death. Second-degree murder. Even if it gets reduced to criminal negligence, treason will get you the chair for sure," said Switzer. "And I'll be there to flip the switch."

"I suppose it doesn't matter one bit that I risked my own life for the government. Clarence's death is on you. The risk was part of the job, and you know it." Wilkens' eyes were wide as he looked at Switzer incredulously.

Switzer stared at him for a moment and just shook his head. Then he stood up, nodding at the guard by the door.

"Lock this scum up."

Chapter Three

The World Government President, Horace Gilani, convened an emergency meeting of his cabinet. He was about to issue an executive order, something that he'd never had to do during his time in office.

All the cabinet officials appeared in the online video monitors.

"I've called this meeting today to discuss our next steps for ensuring this administration's survival. The government needs to deal with the debt payment fiasco and take care of the OCU problem once and for all," said the President.

One of the cabinet ministers, Chalmers, spoke up. "We should have never agreed to such steep concessions for accepting funds from OCU. The terms were ridiculous, and now we have a financial crisis."

"We're past the point of laying blame. You all had a hand in getting us here. I never heard a word of complaint from anyone when you benefited from the extra services and perks the credits bought. Even you, Chalmers. Griping about the situation after agreeing to the conditions in principle doesn't make you a visionary," said President Gilani. "You're as guilty as the rest of us."

"How do you suggest we handle it?" asked Sturgess, another cabinet minister.

"I propose an executive order to halt the concessions to OCU. That should buy us the time necessary to get this written into law. It shouldn't be hard to convince the Senate and the House to agree." Gilani made sure he looked each cabinet minister in the eye to ensure compliance with his wishes. "It's time to vote now. No debate or delays."

Before the votes could be tallied and announced, there was a tussle at the door. The cabinet officials reacted to similar disturbances in their respective offices. Then the video feeds cut out, and the screens went blank.

A contingent of OCU agents entered and surrounded the President.

"What's the meaning of this intrusion?" Gilani asked.

"Sir, I apologize for the interruption. I am Agent Larsen. We are placing you under arrest for the illegal act of subverting Protocol Nine." Larsen held up a tablet and replayed a recording of President Gilani proposing the executive order.

"Place your hands behind your back, please," ordered the agent.

"Do you know who you're addressing?" asked the President. "I'll have you in a cell so small, it'll be standing room only."

Agent Larsen decked the President and pinned him to the table. Another agent yanked his hands behind his back and slapped on a pair of handcuffs.

<<<>>>

Monica Franchette, the MF Overlord, sat fixated on her computer monitor, uttering a gasp every so often. News on the *coup d'état* unfolded over the day. The live streaming events were fed continuously from the many government cameras placed throughout the buildings.

The mainframe room where she holed up was insulated from the chaos. The bank of black mainframe computers hummed along quietly in the cool climate-controlled environment as if the world remained in stasis. They gave no indication of the madness surrounding them or the dire situations occurring in the other governmental departments.

From what Franchette could tell, the OCU forces concentrated their efforts on systems-related activities where the monumental viral attack was successful. It became obvious to her that the OCU overseers had set rules of engagement and were careful not to overstep their reach. Such rules would be smart, in case there was any doubt about what they were doing. If OCU had approached the take-over with uncontrolled aggression, it would have instigated a civil war.

Suddenly there was a banging at the door. Franchette looked up from her screen and glanced at her underling, Craig. He looked up at the same time, and they locked eyes in fear.

Another loud banging rattled the door. "Open up. This is Captain Orrick Smithers of the OCU Containment Brigade. We know you're in there. I repeat, open up at once, or we're breaking in."

Franchette tilted her head toward the door, signaling Craig to open it. Craig reluctantly got up and headed for the door. He unlocked it, letting a small security force of six intimidatingly armed soldiers into the room. They entered with weapons drawn.

A voice boomed out from the rear. "Stand down!"

The armed contingent lowered their rifles. The leader walked past the tight group and paused.

"I am Captain Smithers. Who is in charge here?" He stared down the only two unarmed people in the room.

Franchette stepped forward. "I am. You have no right to be here." She held her ground nervously, wondering whether taking the confrontational response was a wise move.

Smithers looked at her and frowned. "I will decide whether I have the right to be here or not." He glanced back to one of the soldiers in the rear. "Johannson. What do you have for me?"

Private Johannson ran to the Captain, pulling out a tablet from his side pouch. "Sir, it doesn't look like this part of the system was affected by the virus."

"What are you telling me? That Protocol-9 doesn't apply here?" asked Smithers.

"No, sir. This is the only part of the system that P-9 can't touch. Only the systems that the virus affected apply to Protocol-9," said Johannson.

Smithers looked perplexed. "Hmm. That is odd. I was assured we had full rights under the terms of engagement. Why wasn't this part of the system affected?"

Franchette cleared her throat. "Don't be surprised. My department is immune to those types of viral attacks. I stake my life on it." She stepped back and swept her arm toward the bank of L-KATs, affectionately dubbed her Hell-Kats.

The Captain walked past Franchette toward the mainframes. The machines continued to hum steadily. He inspected them visually, his arms behind his back as if he was afraid the equipment would break under his touch.

He was also aware that Franchette kept her eyes on him, ready to pounce if he made so much as a threatening gesture toward the bank of servers. He intuitively knew better than to upset the protective mother-bear.

The MF Overlord waited quietly, turmoil and fear eating her insides until Smithers was satisfied.

The Captain returned to his contingent, shoulders lowered, head bowed. "Fascinating." He turned to his adjutant. "Johannson, make a note. This area is to be designated as a safe zone from here on out. No further action required."

"Are you sure, sir?" The private hesitated before making the note. This was a first for him.

"Yes, damn it. P-9 is very clear and concise. There is no grey area here," said Smithers. There was an element of irritation in his voice.

"Yes, sir." Johannson typed into his tablet, and it made a short melodic chime. "This zone has now been noted as safe and locked."

"Very good." Smithers turned toward Franchette and said, "Sorry to have disturbed you. Carry on." Then he turned toward his team and said, "Fall out. Prepare for the next sector."

The armed contingent filed out of the room, quickly and quietly. Smithers glanced back at Franchette and Craig with a sheepish smile and closed the door behind him.

Chapter Four

Wilkens was abruptly woken up from a deep sleep. It came as a surprise to him.

Not again.

One guard handed him dark overalls to change into.

Now, this is different.

They cuffed his hands and led him out, but they didn't go the regular route. They took him through passages of the prison that he had never seen before. It was obvious the route was not used very often. He could smell mold and moisture. All around him the metal bars and structures were rusted. They must have been in the basement corridor going somewhere secret, away from prying eyes.

Eventually, the two guards led him to a large delivery door in the back of the prison. They rolled up the door, and a dark transport van was waiting. It had been waiting there for a while because Wilkens could smell the buildup of fumes from the vehicle's exhaust. It was old school, using that kind of vehicle. Who used combustion engines these days? Most vehicles were electric.

After the last global war, the world switched over from combustion engines. Gasoline became very cheap, free even because no one used it anymore. Vast stores of surplus fuel sat in long forgotten tanks.

This must be something clandestine.

An old combustion engine vehicle was something that was untraceable back to its owner, the records of ownership having been purged many years ago.

While he pondered the purpose for secrecy, the side door of the transport vehicle popped open, and an armed escort came out, barking to the guards, "What are you waiting for? Load him in."

Wilkens' handcuffs were released, and he was gently escorted into the vehicle. He took a seat on one of the benches without being restrained. There were two other armed escorts within the van, keeping an eye on him.

"Where are you taking me?" asked Wilkens.

The escorts remained silent. The door to the van closed, and Wilkens felt the vehicle move. The ride was uneventful for the rest of what seemed like a long journey. He thought they were going through a lot of trouble just to get rid of him.

Almost immediately after the vehicle stopped, he heard a cacophony of footsteps right before the side door of the van slid open. A team of armed escorts motioned with raised weapons for Wilkens to get out.

One of the men outside lowered his gun, looked at Wilkens, and said, "Follow us, please." When Wilkens nodded and rose slowly, the rest of the guards lowered their guns as well. The civility of this new group of people surprised Wilkens.

He followed without question, but Wilkens was getting a bit concerned as to where they were going. Though it was still dark outside, he saw a large building that appeared abandoned. Some of the windows were shattered. The surrounding neighborhood seemed deserted. They led him inside and down to the basement of the building.

The environment was similar to the unused portion of the prison where he had just come from. He heard dripping water echoing in the distance as they walked through puddles along the cracked concrete floor. The guards may be civil, but the atmosphere was not.

They entered a large chamber and sat him on a chair in front of a typical interrogation table. This was something Wilkens was familiar with. It seemed like he was always sitting on a chair by a table. To top things off, he recognized the figure on the other side. It was Felix Switzer. Except he wasn't dressed in his usual business attire. Switzer wore a dark sweatshirt and baggy pants. He looked defeated, almost pathetic. This did not bode well, Wilkens thought.

One of the armed men placed a hot cup of black coffee on the table in front of Wilkens.

"What is this?" asked Wilkens. "Why the cloak and dagger?" He picked up the steaming coffee and took a sip. *Nirvana.* The soothing beverage took the edge off his nerves.

Switzer took a sip of coffee from his own cup before replying, "The President, or should I say, the ex-President felt the need to make things right," said Switzer. "He apologizes for your treatment and realizes you may be the only way to find out who was behind the viral attack in the Government. He is asking for your assistance."

Wilkens shook his head. "Why should I help you? All I've gotten out of helping this government is the shaft, over and over again. Let's just say there are some serious trust issues at play here. Enough is enough, I think."

"It's not a matter of trust anymore," said Switzer. "The government you know no longer exists. And you hold the key to finding out what happened."

"Why me?" asked Wilkens. "I'm sure there are others who ex-President Gilani trusts. Even you. Aren't you his go-to golden child? Why don't you do the dirty work for him? The work I've done for the World Government has been nothing but trouble for me."

"It's against my better judgment, but odd as it may sound, he *trusts* you. The downfall of the government was a result of deep infiltration by OCU," said Switzer. "We know that you have no ties with them. And there are those who believe you have integrity."

"What would it serve now?" asked Wilkens. "The World Government is now defunct. How can I reverse that?"

"This coup is illegal," said Switzer. "It can only survive if people feel it is right. By exposing OCU's plot, President Gilani hopes that citizens will revolt and reestablish the World Government under his leadership."

"That's a pipe dream," said Wilkens. "Besides, if OCU was powerful enough to take over the government, what chance do I have? I'll be putting a target on my back."

"Yes, we understand that. That's why we're willing to compensate you with a sizable amount of ByteNuggets. As you know, that currency transcends governments and coups. Payment will be made through a third-party payment service, PayRight. I can show you proof that the funds are being held in escrow for you, to be paid out only after you complete the task."

Switzer tapped on his tablet and passed it to Wilkens. Wilkens' eyes widened as he saw the outrageously enormous amount of ByteNuggets sitting in an account, ready for transfer to him.

Switzer continued, "With those funds, you can start a new life. Change your face, move your family, go into hiding. Whatever you want. Even OCU wouldn't be able to find you. You can buy your own island and live there for the rest of your life. Just get this one little task done first."

Wilkens sat there, contemplating what he was hearing. A new lease on life just opened up for him. But at what cost? He would end up having to watch his back for the rest of his life if he took their deal. The pros and cons were bombarding his brain, and he didn't know what to do.

"I won't insult you by appealing to your sense of patriotism. We have failed you as a government. You only have two choices," said Switzer. "Either find out who was responsible for the viral attack and be well compensated or you can just walk away and live the rest of your life in obscurity. Either way, you are free now. It's your choice."

Switzer left the tablet on the table. He stood up, walked to the exit and paused. Turning back toward Wilkens, he said, "Connect the dots, expose OCU's involvement." Then he disappeared into the dark passageway, the rest of his security detail following behind.

Wilkens remained seated, staring at the tablet.

Chapter Five

Due to the dissolving of the World Government, the only evidence that it ever existed was the small, seemingly insignificant department run by the MF Overlord.

As it was, Franchette was expected to attend department head meetings and run the World Government system for OCU. Under the lease agreement, OCU would be able to access the database from the mainframes on a piecemeal basis.

The MF Overlord's responsibility was to ensure the mainframes ran smoothly during and after the transition.

Finally!

After so many years, hidden within the shadow of the server farm overlords, Franchette and her beloved bank of machines were getting the recognition she believed they deserved. Her far superior army of mainframes had repelled the viral attack that took down the World Government's entire systems network of vulnerable server farms. Her department had survived the recent government upheaval, and if she played her cards right, it would survive its new iteration, whatever that may be, going forward.

She and her team were safe, for now.

<<◇>>

The plane took off with very little fanfare. From the tarmac, there was no indication that it contained the highest officials, including the President, of the former World Government.

President Gilani was still awaiting news of a scandal from Switzer. Little did he know, but Switzer had already lost contact with his operative, Wilkens, who was tasked to uncover the source behind the attacks on the Government's computer systems. If a conspiracy was revealed, perhaps it could be used to reverse the hold that OCU had over the World Government and forgive the missed payments.

The plane taxied to the runway and then accelerated to gain lift. Gilani held his breath for what seemed like several minutes. He knew the most likely occurrences for air accidents to happen was during take-off and landing. The plane maintained a steep ascent and made a wide sweeping course adjustment in under fifty seconds. Gilani released his breath in relief. It would be hours before the plane was scheduled to land.

He survived the first occurrence and could relax over the next few hours. There was nothing he could do in the meantime. Where they were headed, he had no idea. Communications access was limited for security reasons, and he had no idea what was and wasn't working. The only thing he could do was hope for the best, which seemed dismal at present.

Chapter Six

Wilkens pored over the software analysis data. He checked the operating system that the server farms used as the backbone of the World Government's computer systems. Doing a line-by-line comparison, he discovered an anomaly that disturbed him.

He had built a backdoor to all his software applications, as he was the original designer of the program. But the backdoor contained an additional subroutine that was beautifully crafted in that it was able to cover its tracks after making crucial alterations.

Coding had a simplistic beauty that few recognized and even fewer appreciated. It was an artform, and coding artists like Wilkens appreciated the creativity that goes into each masterpiece.

Wilkens called up the secret log for the backdoor access and discovered that there were innumerable incursions. Each incursion made minute changes in the code that wasn't significant enough to be detected. But over many years, the overall effect compromised the entire server farm. Someone was playing the long game, and they had a head start.

The end result was that the computer system became vulnerable to a sniper-wipe. All that was needed was the addition of a pro-virus to activate a cascade effect, and the whole system came crashing down like an avalanche. This was what distinguished it as a masterpiece as opposed to just another hack.

All the files were purged from the regular server farm. Wilkens performed a virtual tour of the affected system for clues. He donned the equipment that he used when he destroyed BugzE, the mother virus that had killed Clarence. But this time, he was by himself. There would be no one to pull him out in case of a problem. It wasn't the brightest of ideas, but it was all Wilkens had.

Once inside the system, Wilkens looked in every direction, in every shadow. Before, when they were hunting down BugzE, there were definite passages and hallways and a lot of infrastructure of the various system applications and subroutines.

Now, it was just an empty chamber with no discernible walls. Floating about were bits of red dust, fragments of the virus code that had since been taken apart. Other vestiges of the former program were aimlessly drifting about.

The entire system had performed an automatic reboot and reconfiguration after the debt payments were missed. Wilkens didn't have any proof, just his gut feeling, but he knew somehow that OCU was involved.

Virtual Sentient Technologies (VST) had won the lucrative contract to supply and service the World Government's computer network system, with the exception of the original mainframe system,

Franchette's babies. It was his job to find the connection between VST and OCU.

Wilkens could see the new structure take shape as the computer system rebuilt itself. There was nothing more for him to find. In a few hours, the network would have completed its restructuring program.

Leaving the system, Wilkens decided to try a different tact. On the Government directory was the Records Department, where he found an area called Archives. Perhaps the old records will yield a clue, something that he desperately needed.

<<<>>>

The Archives area was located in a little-used building, separate from the main governmental offices. It was a large building, one Wilkens remembered passing almost every day, not knowing what its true function was until now.

He entered the building, which was eerily quiet. From the directory, he located the information desk. It wasn't that obvious, which was strange, given this was the place where physical records and information were stored.

Wilkens approached the desk, that was more like a window, similar to what a bank teller would be standing behind. But no one was around. On the ledge was a bell with a sign. It read – *Ring for Service*. Wilkens gave the bell a quick two-tap hit. It rang out twice. In the background, he could hear shuffling.

"Be right with you, dear."

A moment later, an older woman appeared. She was bent over and walked as if each step was torture, yet she used no cane. She looked as old as the dull and tarnished fixtures in the building.

"How may I help you?" she asked when she finally reached the window.

"I'm looking for some information," said Wilkens, suddenly feeling stupid for stating the obvious.

The woman ignored the faux pas, but her eyes held a bored look as if to say, "So what else is new?"

"I mean, I'd like to know what kind of records are stored here?" Wilkens felt a bit better with the new start.

"Oh, my. You must be new."

"I suppose you don't get very many visitors?" asked Wilkens.

"No, you're right, dear. Only historians. And only a few times a year." The woman drew forth a visitor log. "Sign here, please."

Wilkens chuckled as he grabbed a chewed-up pen from the penholder. This was so old school.

As he signed the visitor log, the woman said, "The records are hard copies. From before everything went digital."

"How far back does it go?" asked Wilkens.

"The most recent physical records are at least twenty years old now, dear."

"Nothing more recent?" asked Wilkens.

"No. Once the system went digital, everything was backed up in the electronic systems."

"Does that mean the recent virus wouldn't have affected anything here?"

"My, aren't you the little genius," said the woman.

Feeling a bit chagrined, Wilkens continued. "If the government stopped keeping hard copies of records, why is this all still here? Why are you still around?"

"Silly man. It wasn't in the budget to digitize everything all at once. The records here are kept for fifty years. We have another thirty years to go before all the records are destroyed. I'm afraid that will be after my time."

"What happens to the older records after fifty years?"

"Those records are digitized before they are destroyed."

"You're telling me that the oldest records here are fifty years old."

"Well, that was the theory. Budget cuts and staff layoffs have thrown a wrench in the works. As a cost-cutting measure, destruction of the older records was halted. In fact, we are storing records that are much older than we would normally. Who knows what you'll find down there now." The old woman let out a short cackle as if laughing at a private joke. "Was there anything in particular that you wanted to see?"

"Yes, I want to locate the earliest records available for OmniClon Universal and its registration for incorporation." Wilkens didn't feel hopeful, but he had to explore all avenues.

"Let me check. Yes, those records are in the Archives. Here is the call number for it. ZLS-149. Here is a map of where the sections are located. If you have trouble finding anything, just use the intercom system on each floor. They all reroute back to me up here."

"Thank you for your help." Wilkens went to the subfloor sections to locate the records. He was able to find the articles of incorporation for OCU. But there were no documents for VST. The corporation must have formed after the system switched over to digital.

Wilkens returned to the information desk.

"Did you find everything you needed?" asked the woman.

"No, I couldn't locate any documents regarding Virtual Sentient Technologies."

"Have you tried the mainframes?" asked the woman.

"No, why would I do that?" asked Wilkens.

"You never know, young man. The mainframes were initially used to back up all the Government records until they upgraded to that snazzy new system."

Wilkens was surprised by what he heard. It was a long shot, but he had nothing else to go on. He braced himself for the visit. The MF Overlord's reputation preceded her, and Wilkens had no interest in becoming cannon fodder.

Chapter Seven

"No fucking way are you going to touch my babies!" yelled Franchette.

"Look, you would be doing me a solid," said Wilkens. "If there's anything I can do for you in return, let me know."

Franchette paused for a moment to consider. This was Wilkens, and she had heard the stories of his exploits. He was the talk of the town, and everybody considered him a hero.

She had always wanted to dine at *Le Chateau*, having heard the filet mignon was to die for. But she was never able to get reservations. The fact she found Wilkens rather cute was an added bonus. When he offered to do anything for her, she couldn't resist.

"There is one thing you can do for me. That is if you're up to the challenge," said Franchette suggestively.

"Try me," said Wilkens.

"I'll let you peek in my mainframes in exchange for dinner at *Le Chateau*," said Franchette.

Wilkens paused. He was caught by surprise. He had always kept a respectful distance from the MF Overlord because of her reputation. She was attractive in her own way, but he never thought a guy like him would appeal to a woman like her. But this new development intrigued him. He often dined at *Le Chateau*, and never had a problem getting his favorite table.

"Hell, if you find what I'm looking for, I'll throw in a limo ride, to and from the restaurant," he said before she could change her mind.

"You let me sneak a peek under your drawers and dinner is on me," said Wilkens.

Franchette almost seemed to purr as she reached out and caressed his face. "I like how you think. Grrrr."

Although Franchette allowed Wilkens access to the mainframe, that didn't mean he was allowed to sit at the workstation of the mainframe and do whatever he wanted. He had to tell Franchette what he wanted, and she would input the search query. That didn't surprise him at all. If they ever did get to go out to dinner, he planned to order for her and let her idly watch him do it. Let's see how she liked that.

Wilkens had no high hopes of finding any helpful or revealing results. It didn't seem worth it, the price he had to pay to get at information that was potentially non-existent. Franchette worked in silence, mumbling search combination queries to herself every so often. He remained seated beside Franchette, fidgeting with his tablet for what seemed like an eternity when she finally spoke.

"There's nothing here."

Wilkens lowered his tablet and slumped in the seat. "You found nothing?"

"I've searched high and low. If there were any documents with a hint of OCU or VST in them, I would have found them. The only thing that shows up is a folder of corporate party pics." Franchette clicked on the folder and browsed through the images. "Team building shit, that sort of stuff."

Franchette continued to browse through the albums as Wilkens contemplated his next move, glancing over at the pictures every so often.

Suddenly, one of the images that flashed by caught his eye. "Wait!"

"What? What did you see?" asked Franchette as she paused her browsing.

"Go back."

She went back slowly through the photos in reverse order, one by one, stopping sporadically at what she thought was the image Wilkens wanted.

"Nope. Keep going. I'll tell you when to stop," said Wilkens in an impatient tone.

Franchette continued on, examining the photos as they lit up the screen.

"Stop," exclaimed Wilkens. His face lit up with excitement.

Franchette looked at the picture, and all she could see was a handful of young men and women in a group shot. It was an old photo, and the only person she recognized was a young Allistar Cruikshank, the CEO of OCU. "What's so special about this picture?"

"This is our smoking gun. Don't you see? It's the connection between OCU and VST." He pointed at the figure of one of the gentlemen in the photo. "That there is the CEO of VST, Charles Rendall."

Wilkens recognized many others as well. There were top OCU officials and CEOs of OCU's other known and unknown subsidiaries.

At that moment, it all became clear to Wilkens. He surmised that the only way a backdoor subroutine could have been added to affect the government's computer system on such a global level was if it was sanctioned at the top corporate level. At Charles Rendall's level.

VST ensured that the system would halt, based on the program parameters that the mother company, OCU, had decreed. Unbeknownst to the world, OCU had pulled the strings of the various smaller corporations that had government contracts in critical areas and functions. OCU made sure of that. Even the World Government security protocols were developed by an outside firm that had hidden ties with OCU.

Wilkens recognized the various figures in the image. They were all CEOs of different high-tech companies, most with no known affiliation with OCU. But this photo proved otherwise.

That was how OCU was able to keep close tabs on what the President and his cabinet were about to do with the executive order. As soon as certain keywords were uttered, it activated a recording to capture the moment for evidence.

Of course, OCU had anticipated the government's actions and had their forces ready to take action simultaneously across the globe in each minister's government office.

Wilkens knew he couldn't get close to OCU's CEO, Allistar Cruikshank, without exposing himself at great risk. His next best choice would be to confront the CEO of VST, Charles Rendall, who would know more about the possibilities for sabotage. Wilkens slapped the table, put on his coat and headed toward the door.

"Hey, wait a minute. What about dinner?" yelled Franchette, before Wilkens could make his escape.

"Oh, we're on. I've already got a wine picked out," Wilkens yelled back.

The thought of dinner with the sultry MF Overlord flashed briefly through his mind, but at that moment, he had a more pressing issue to deal with. Time to visit the VST head office.

"I'm investigating the incident of the virus that attacked the World Government computer systems, and

I need to speak to Charles Rendall, your CEO," asked Wilkens.

The receptionist looked up at Wilkens as if she had seen a ghost. She stopped her typing and straightened her shirt. Clearing her throat, she said, "I'm afraid to inform you that Mr. Rendall recently passed on."

Wilkens did a double take and paused to let the information sink in. "What do you mean, he passed on? When did this happen?"

"Believe me. We're as surprised as you are."

"How did he die?"

"They found him this morning in his penthouse suite." The receptionist paused and looked around to see if anyone was listening. Then she whispered, "Rumor has it, they think it was a heart attack, but the results of the autopsy still need to be determined and announced. You didn't hear it from me."

"Thank you for your time," said Wilkens. This was a dead-end, but it seemed suspicious. He considered visiting the morgue, but knew he could just hack into the government system to find out everything he needed. Also, he didn't like the thought of examining a dead body. Better to leave that to the experts. They had stronger stomachs.

Instead, he made a detour to his warehouse to pick up some equipment before heading to Rendall's penthouse. It might still be cordoned off from visitors so he could work in peace. Wilkens wasn't sure who he

could trust anymore. Well, except for maybe
Franchette.

When Wilkens arrived at Rendall's penthouse, there
were no barriers to entry. That meant the authorities
didn't suspect any foul play, yet.

Wilkens easily jigged the lock to gain entry.
Everything was clean and tidy. Just the bed was
unmade.

He canvased the unit and thought to himself that
there wasn't anything useful there. His tablet chimed.
He had set it to let him know when an autopsy report
was filed in the coroner's computer system. Perhaps it
would lend a clue as to what he should be looking for.

He accessed the report and scanned it. Time of
death was estimated as 4:40 AM. The deceased was
discovered in the bathroom, on the floor.

*If I were getting up that early, I would also be doing
my daily wake-up morning routine and be in the
bathroom.*

Wilkens checked out the alarm clock and saw that it
was set for a 4:30 AM wakeup chime.

Wilkens entered the bathroom and examined
everything in great detail. A toothbrush was lying in the
sink, the bubbly white residue of what would have been
a mixture of saliva and toothpaste still clinging to the
bristles. Rendall must have been brushing his teeth
when he collapsed.

On a hunch, Wilkens pulled out a device from his backpack. He turned it on and scanned the room. He went over it once quickly and found nothing. Then he decided to do a deeper, more thorough scan by running the device closer to the floor along the baseboards.

The screen lit up on the third pass using a different setting, and an image flashed in bright red. Whatever it was, the image source was located behind the baseboard by the sink. It was buried deep within the wall.

Wilkens removed his backpack and rummaged through it, pulling out a crowbar. With it, he pried back the baseboard and shined his flashlight along the revealed crevice.

He scanned the baseboard again and studied the image. It looked like some sort of bug. From his jacket pocket, he pulled out a pair of forceps and dug around the crevice behind the baseboard.

He pulled out what seemed to be the remains of a cockroach. Except this cockroach looked manufactured. It was a good replica, but its insides were dissolved and coalesced into a minuscule dab of brownish goo.

The scanner showed that the residue contained formic acid. Wilkens pressed a button on the scanner marked <Reconstruct>. Immediately, the scanner software began to create an image based on the remains. As he suspected, the completed image was that of a cockroach.

Wilkens had read of such advanced nanotechnology, but had never heard of it being used in an assassination. There were only a few poisons that would fit the bill. He took a swab and used it to absorb the brown goo from within the bug's exoskeleton.

Just then, he heard the penthouse front door close and footsteps walking around the living room. He quickly stowed the swab in his bag and hid behind the bathroom door. Peeking around the door, he looked at the hall reflection from the bathroom mirror.

A man was searching the apartment, looking for something specific it seemed. He was armed and didn't look friendly. This was not someone Wilkens wanted to run into on the street, much less in an enclosed penthouse with limited exits. Wilkens packed up his gear and waited for an opportunity to escape undetected or at least unharmed.

As the man walked out onto the balcony, Wilkens made his move. He ran to the door, opened it and started to exit. A shot rang out, and something hit the doorjamb by his head. The doorjamb shattered, throwing shards of wood into the right side of Wilkens' face.

The pain caused his right eye to shut tight, and he stumbled sideways, hitting the doorjamb on the other side. Fortunately, it stopped him from collapsing. Blood trickled down his face from the wound. Half-blinded, he ran toward the stairwell by the elevator as two more shots whizzed by, barely missing him.

Just as he approached the door to the stairwell, the elevator dinged.

What timing!

The elevator door had opened by the time he reached it, revealing a group of rowdy convention attendees. They hastily made room for Wilkens, gasping at the sight of his bloodied face and allowing him extra standing room.

Just before the elevator doors closed, Wilkens turned around and saw the dark figure of the would-be killer disappear behind the doorway of the stairwell at the other end of the penthouse floor.

Wilkens had literally dodged those bullets.

Chapter Eight

Monica Franchette arrived at the warehouse after getting off the transit system and walking through a busy shopping complex toward the industrial district. As instructed, she ensured she wasn't followed before ducking into an alleyway. At the third building, she stopped at a faded gray metal door and rang the buzzer. She looked at the camera above the doorway. An electronic latch unlocked, and Franchette pushed the door open.

The hallway was dark, but a dim light at the end other end invited her in.

"I'm in here."

Franchette recognized Wilkens' voice and followed it to the doorway at the end of the hallway.

Wilkens was standing beside a man she didn't recognize, and they were both bent over what looked like a portable spectrometer. Wilkens inserted a sample and looked up.

"Oh, there you are. Just in time."

"Just in time for what?" asked Franchette.

"Just in time for the big reveal," answered Wilkens. There was a hint of playful mischievousness in his voice.

"What happened to your face?" Franchette had noticed the bandage on the right side of Wilkens' face as she approached.

"Oh, this." Wilkens reached up to pat the dry bandage to make sure it was still secure. "I had a run-in with a doorjamb. You should have seen the doorjamb. No biggie."

Franchette gave an obligatory chuckle and motioned nervously toward the stranger beside Wilkens. "Who's your friend?"

Wilkens noticed the worried look on her face. "Oh, yes. Sorry, should have done this sooner." He gestured toward the fellow beside him. "This here is my tech guy, Virgil. He was my secret weapon when I was battling the virus for the World Government."

Virgil gave a short wave of his hand without looking up from the workstation.

Franchette ignored the brisk acknowledgment and studied the high-tech equipment around her. "Your workshop is impressive. I let you peek at my equipment. Maybe you'll let me peek at yours?" She looked at Wilkens with innocent, wide eyes.

Wilkens smirked. "I'm already buying you dinner for the privilege. What else do you have to barter?"

Franchette thrust out her lips in a playful pout. "I have skills."

"I bet you do," said Wilkens, furrowing one brow and raising the other. "Tell you what. If you're good, I'll give you access to my hard drive."

"Geez, you two. Get a room already," said an exasperated Virgil.

The scanner beeped, diverting Wilkens' attention. Virgil looked at the spectrometer screen and typed furiously on his workstation.

"Is this what killed him?" asked Wilkens.

"I've never seen anything like this. I can't identify it" said Virgil. He manipulated the image on the screen to try to find anything familiar with the atomic configuration.

"Can I see it?" asked Franchette.

The two men stepped aside to allow Franchette access to the workstation. She typed in a few commands and pulled out a tablet from her bag.

"I'm sending the data to my tablet. I can use my VPN to access the mainframes. If they can't identify the compound, then nothing else will." Franchette opened a gateway on her tablet and typed in a query string.

A few moments later, her tablet beeped. Franchette read the result out loud, "It's a derivative of a substance known as Compound B-184."

"Compound B-184?" asked Wilkens, all of a sudden alert.

"Why? Does that mean something to you?" asked Franchette, her brows furrowed with puzzlement.

"I'm familiar with it, too," said Virgil. "Remember those stories about it being used as a household insecticide? Anyway, it was banned many years ago due to a high incidence of coronary accidents. The link would never have been discovered if it wasn't for the works of Dr. Meinschott and his longitudinal cohort study."

"Yes," said Wilkens. "And the company selling the pesticide filed for bankruptcy. AgrariTech was the name. OCU saved the company by buying it for cheap. The CEO for that company was also in the picture we found in the mainframe."

It was a light-bulb moment for all three, hitting them at the same time.

"We know that VST was behind the faulty server farm system that brought down the World Government. VST's CEO, Charles Rendall, was assassinated, his death made to look like he died of natural causes." Wilkens looked at Franchette and paused.

"We can connect the assassination of Charles Rendall to OCU with the weaponized version of Compound B-184," said Franchette. "Will that be enough?"

"It might be enough to raise serious questions and open an inquiry," said Wilkens.

"I wouldn't hold my breath," said Virgil. He increased the volume of the news flash that was playing on the media console.

...when the plane hit the side of a mountain. The rescue operation has been downgraded to recovery status. I repeat. The plane carrying the President of the former World Government and other high-level officials has crashed with no survivors. The cause is believed to be an instrument malfunction...

Wilkens couldn't believe his ears. He didn't know whether to be happy or sad. Was he home free or did he have a different target on his back? Now that he knew the truth, who would he tell it to?

As far as he knew, there was only one obligation left to fulfill.

Chapter Nine

The limousine pulled up in front of Monica Franchette's apartment building where she had stepped out only moments before. She felt uncomfortable in her high heels and low-neck black dress, attire that she was not used to wearing. Her perfume wafted gently in the light breeze of the early evening.

Very impressive. He really went all out. The door of the black limousine opened, and out stepped Wilkens.

"Well, what do you think?" Wilkens looked at her expectantly with wide puppy-dog eyes, as if asking for approval.

"I must say, I'm impressed. Well done," said Franchette. She blushed at the thought of what was to come for the rest of the evening if this was any indication of how things were going so far.

Wilkens waited by the open door for Franchette as she approached the vehicle. He held his hand out and led her inside. Like the gentleman that he was, he closed the door, went around to the other side and got in. Franchette had never been in such a fancy ride before. They both enjoyed the trip over to the restaurant, making small talk as the conversation progressed toward a more intimate one.

Dinner was at the fancy restaurant, *Le Chateau*, at the top of the SkyLine building, a place that Franchette had always wanted to go to but thought she could never afford.

"How did you manage to get reservations to this place?" asked Franchette. "I've heard it gets booked solid for months. To be honest, I never thought you'd be able to pull it off."

"Let's just say I know a guy, who knows a guy. I can't reveal all my secrets. Besides, I'm already going to let you look at my hardware," said Wilkens.

Franchette's pupils dilated as Wilkens transformed before her mind's eye into a mysterious man who had many secrets. It was something that she was not able to control, and it showed. Wilkens looked at her with penetrating eyes, as if he knew her very thoughts. It scared her while exciting her at the same time.

The waiter arrived and set up a small table complete with carving service. Franchette looked at Wilkens questioningly.

"I took the liberty of ordering for us ahead of time. This dish requires two hours of preparation. I hope you like duck," said Wilkens.

Duck! How in the world could he afford that?

Franchette blushed again. "Yes, yes. Duck is fine. This is way beyond what I expected. I've actually never had duck before," said Franchette.

"I had it one other time and loved it. It is a taste that more people should experience," said Wilkens.

The waiter expertly carved the crisp duck into thin slices. He then placed the slices onto rice wraps, garnishing them with fresh slivers of spring onion, cucumber, and a dollop of sweet bean sauce on top.

"You eat these with your hands," said Wilkens. He rolled up a wrap with his fingers and took a bite.

Observing what Wilkens did, Franchette copied his actions and took a bite of the duck wrap. "Mmmm. I've never tasted anything so exquisite."

Wilkens watched as some of the juice from the moist duck dripped from her lips.

Franchette noticed him staring at her with lusting eyes. "Your look is revealing what you're thinking. And it rhymes with duck." She put her half-eaten wrap down and licked her finger slowly.

Wilkens grinned and handed her a napkin. "Don't get too full on this. More courses to come," said Wilkens.

The rest of dinner was just as lavish, with Franchette enjoying every dish for the very first time. She never thought food could taste this good.

After their fine dining experience and two bottles of a respectable wine, Franchette was justifiably enchanted and feeling frisky. They left the restaurant where a different limo awaited them.

"I have another surprise for you," said Wilkens.

He looked at her and gave her a sly smile. As he opened the door to the limo, Franchette could see flashing lights and heard music playing inside. She took Wilkens' hand as he led her inside. In the middle of the limousine was a dance pole. Franchette, having taken lessons in the art of pole dancing, gravitated toward it immediately.

"How did you know?" she asked, as she swung around the pole with one hand. It didn't matter that she was in a dress with a low-cut chest line. Not waiting for Wilkens to answer, she grabbed the pole with both hands and started gyrating along its length. Wilkens had already gotten into the limo and sat back to watch as she gave him the show of his lifetime.

Just as the limo arrived at the hotel, Wilkens' tablet beeped. The message made his heart skip a beat. The transfer of ByteNuggets had completed automatically, and he was suddenly a very rich man. With ex-President Gilani dead, there was no one to cancel the pending credit transfer, which proceeded as if he had completed his mission.

Bureaucrats! Gotta love them.

This was the only time he had ever benefited from their mistakes, and there was no longer a World Government that could claw the payment back.

"What was the message? Why do you look like you got away with something?" asked Franchette as she settled down beside him.

"Let's just say everything I've been through up to this point has been worth it." Wilkens put his arm around Franchette's waist and pulled her in for a kiss.

The Next Morning

A double knock sounded at the suite door. "Room service," came a voice from the hallway outside.

Wilkens pulled the covers back, looking over at Franchette. She was still sleeping.

"Breakfast is here. I'll get it," he said.

Wilkens rose from the bed to answer the door. The server pushed in the dining cart containing two covered platters, silverware, orange juice, and coffee. Wilkens uncovered one of the platters and inhaled deeply.

"Mmmm. Nothing like Eggs Benedict in the morning after a night of rigorous exercise."

"Will that be all, sir?" asked the server.

"Yes. Thank you very much," said Wilkens as he handed over a credit chit as a tip.

"Much obliged. You have a nice day," said the server with a grin as he looked over at the naked Franchette, who was still sleeping.

After the service attendant left, Wilkens poured a fresh cup of coffee and brought it over to Franchette. He wafted the hot cup under her nose. Franchette stirred and then opened her eyes. When she saw the cup of coffee, she cracked a small smile.

"That smells good. Did you order us breakfast?" asked Franchette, as she lifted her head to see the dining cart full of food. "You are so sweet."

Wilkens put the coffee down on the bedside table and leaned over to plant a kiss on her cheek. Franchette shifted so that her lips locked onto his. One thing led to another while their breakfasts remained on the cart, getting cold.

While the enamored couple ignored the universe, two cockroaches skittered out from beneath the dining cart onto the carpet and headed toward the bathroom.

-The End-

If you enjoyed this title, I would appreciate your leaving a review of the book. Good reviews encourage an author to write as well as help books to sell. Good reviews can be just a few short sentences describing what you liked about the book without having a spoiler. If you could spend 30 seconds writing a review, I would appreciate it: you can review this title right now at your favorite retailer.

Here is a preview of **another story** you may enjoy:

Year 2428 at the Free Humanity Movement (FHM) Headquarters (50 Years Post-ka'Thar World Invasion)

THE EXPLOSION resonated throughout the cavernous chamber, raining chunks of the ceiling, some large enough to kill, on the fleeing staff below. Thankfully, most of the personnel were gone, having been forewarned only moments before.

Sonia was not so lucky. A chunk of rock, deflecting from the side of the chamber in an altered trajectory, struck her squarely on the head. She collapsed on the cavern floor, unnoticed, while others rushed around in panic mode.

Nobody thought to check on Sonia.

When she came to, she realized she'd only been out for a few minutes, judging by the continued commotion. The first thing she noticed was heavy dust in her mouth and nostrils from the broken concrete surrounding her, pieces of the once protective walls and ceiling changed now into weapons. Dry particles stung her eyes causing tears to flow, blurring her vision further. She wiped her face with a chalky-covered hand, making it worse. By the time her senses had returned, Carson, the unit supervisor, had spotted her and yelled for a medic. Both he and the medic made their way to her, dodging the debris on the littered floor.

She staggered to her feet and swayed for a moment before leaning against the wall for support. Glancing around, she saw others in rougher shape than she and waved the medic away. "Please, attend to her first." She pointed to Camille, one of the maintenance crew, who was bleeding from a head wound. While the medic went to check on Camille, Carson gave Sonia a quick once over before letting her go.

Sonia probed her head with tentative fingers, confirming a massive bump, and blinking against the pain. *I've had worse. I'll live.* She pushed off from the wall with shaking arms and stumbled a few steps. Pausing for a moment to regain her composure, she walked on unsure feet toward the briefing room and her father, Commander Garon Rogal. He'd be wondering where she was, worried about her condition.

"There you are," said Commander Rogal. He looked at Sonia then glanced quickly away. She could tell he was struggling to keep an unconcerned expression on his face. Her disheveled appearance and a scrape on her forehead didn't help matters but she knew he wouldn't comment. Sonia had a tough enough time proving herself to her peers without the top commander of the Free Humanity Movement (FHM) showing favoritism, even if it meant putting her in harm's way.

"Sorry for the delay," said Sonia. "Nothing I couldn't handle. They're getting close."

"There's a bigger issue at hand," said Rogal. "We're about to begin the briefing. Please take a seat."

Sonia grabbed one of the few empty seats near the front and gingerly eased her into it. On the screen behind Rogal, a recording of the security feed showed the attack from outside. A bright flash from the display caused Sonia to squint her eyes and then the feed went dead. Big red letters flashed across the screen.

Enemy attackers identified—OmniClon Universal Attack Forces.

Sonia found this amusing, despite the annoying ache in her head. Of course, this was the work of the OCU. *Who else would it be?*

If you enjoyed this sample then look for **Tomorrow's Past: The Time Guardian Thriller Series - Book 1**.

Other Books by Freddie Kim

- The Time Guardian Thriller Series

- Stinger Jacked

Get the latest update on new releases from the author at:

https://www.freddiekim.com/newsletter/

About the Author - Freddie Kim

As a child, Freddie Kim would make blanket forts and refrigerator-box space ships, both essential things needed to repel against invasion from an alien race. Freddie has never really grown up from his childhood fantasies. The inspiration that he draws from the memories of his youth is captured and revealed to all in his writing.

Connect with Freddie Kim

I really appreciate you reading my book! Here are my social media coordinates:

Friend me on Facebook:
https://www.facebook.com/FreddieKimAuthor/

Follow me on Twitter:
https://twitter.com/freddiekimauth1

Check me out on Goodreads:
https://www.goodreads.com/author/show/16961603.Freddie_Kim

Subscribe to my newsletter:
https://www.freddiekim.com/newsletter/

Visit my website: https://www.freddiekim.com/

* 9 7 8 1 7 7 3 5 0 0 7 7 5 *